THE RAILROAD AND THE CHURCHYARD

AND

THE FATHER

Two Stories

BY

BJÖRNSTJERNE BJÖRNSON

BJÖRNSTJERNE BJÖRNSON

THE RAILROAD AND THE CHURCHYARD
AND
THE FATHER

Two Stories

BY

BJÖRNSTJERNE BJÖRNSON

Fredonia Books
Amsterdam, The Netherlands

The Railroad and the Churchyard and The Father
(Two Stories)

by
Björnstjerne Björnson

ISBN: 1-4101-0772-8

Fredonia Books
Amsterdam, The Netherlands
http://www.fredoniabooks.com

THE RAILROAD AND THE
CHURCHYARD

BY

BJÖRNSTJERNE BJÖRNSON

Translated by Carl Larsen.

THE RAILROAD AND THE CHURCH-
YARD

I.

CANUTE AAKRE belonged to an ancient
family of the parish, where it had always
been distinguished for its intelligence and care
for the public good. His father through self-ex-
ertion had attained to the ministry, but had died
early, and his widow being by birth a peasant,
the children were brought up as farmers. Consequently, Canute's education was only of the
kind afforded by the public school; but his
father's library had early inspired him with a
desire for knowledge, which was increased by
association with his friend Henrik Wergeland,
who often visited him or sent him books, seeds
for his farm, and much good counsel. Agree-
ably to his advice, Canute early got up a club for
practice in debating and study of the constitu-
tion, but which finally became a practical agri-
cultural society, for this and the surrounding
parishes. He also established a parish library,

3

giving his father's books as its first endowment, and organized in his own house a Sunday-school for persons wishing to learn penmanship, arithmetic, and history. In this way the attention of the public was fixed upon him, and he was chosen a member of the board of parish-commissioners, of which he soon became chairman. Here he continued his endeavors to advance the school interests, which he succeeded in placing in an admirable condition.

Canute Aakre was a short-built, active man, with small sharp eyes and disorderly hair. He had large lips which seemed constantly working, and a row of excellent teeth which had the same appearance, for they shone when he spoke his clear sharp words, which came out with a snap, as when the sparks are emitted from a great fire.

Among the many he had helped to an education, his neighbor Lars Hogstad stood foremost. Lars was not much younger than Canute, but had developed more slowly. Being in the habit of talking much of what he read and thought, Canute found in Lars—who bore a quiet, earnest manner—a good listener, and step by step a sensible judge. The result was, that he went reluctantly to the meetings of the board, unless first furnished with Lars Hogstad's advice, concerning whatever matter of importance was before it, which matter was thus most likely to result in practical improvement. Canute's influence, therefore, brought his neighbor in as a member of the board, and finally into everything with which he himself was connected. They always rode together to the meetings, where Lars never spoke, and only on the road to and from, could Canute learn his opinion. They were looked upon as inseparable.

One fine autumn day, the parish-commissioners were convened, for the purpose of considering, among other matters, a proposal made by the Foged, to sell the public grain-magazine, and with the proceeds establish a savings-bank. Canute Aakre, the chairman, would certainly have approved this, had he been guided by his better judgment; but, in the first place, the motion was made by the Foged, whom Wergeland did not like, consequently, neither did Canute; secondly, the grain-magazine had been erected by his powerful paternal grandfather, by whom it was presented to the parish. To him the proposal was not free from an appearance of personal offence; therefore, he had not spoken of it to any one, not even to Lars, who never himself introduced a subject.

As chairman, Canute read the proposal without comment, but, according to his habit, looked over to Lars, who sat as usual a little to one side, holding a straw between his teeth; this he

always did when entering upon a subject, using
it as he would a toothpick, letting it hang loosely
in one corner of his mouth, or turning it more
quickly or slowly, according to the humor he was
in. Canute now saw with surprise, that the straw
moved very fast. He asked quickly, " Do you
think we ought to agree to this ? "

Lars answered dryly, " Yes, I do."

The whole assembly, feeling that Canute was
of quite a different opinion, seemed struck, and
looked at Lars, who said nothing further, nor
was further questioned. Canute turned to another subject, as if nothing had happened, and
did not again resume the question till toward the
close of the meeting, when he asked with an air
of indifference if they should send it back to the
Foged for closer consideration, as it certainly
was contrary to the mind of the people of the
parish, by whom the grain-magazine was highly
valued ; also, if he should put upon the record,
" Proposal deemed inexpedient."

" Against one vote," said Lars.

" Against two," said another instantly.

" Against three," said a third, and before the
chairman had recovered from his surprise, a ma-
jority had declared in favor of the proposal.

He wrote ; then read in a low tone, " Referred
for acceptance, and the meeting adjourned."
Canute, rising and closing the " Records,"
blushed deeply, but resolved to have this vote

defeated in the parish meeting. In the yard he hitched his horse to the wagon, and Lars came and seated himself by his side. On the way home they spoke upon various subjects, but not upon this.

On the following day Canute's wife started for Lars' house, to inquire of his wife if anything had happened between their husbands; Canute had appeared so queerly when he returned home the evening previous. A little beyond the house she met Lars' wife, who came to make the same inquiry on account of a similar peculiar behavior in her husband. Lars' wife was a quiet, timid thing, easily frightened, not by hard words, but by silence; for Lars never spoke to her unless she had done wrong, or he feared she would do so. On the contrary, Canute Aakre's wife spoke much with her husband, and particularly about the commissioners' meetings, for lately they had taken his thoughts, work, and love from her and the children. She was jealous of it as of a woman, she wept at night about it, and quarrelled with her husband concerning it in the day. But now she could say nothing; for once he had returned home unhappy; she immediately became much more so than he, and for the life of her she must know what was the matter. So as Lars' wife could tell her nothing, she had to go for information out in the parish, where she obtained it, and of course was instantly of her husband's opinion, thinking Lars incomprehensible, not to say bad. But when she let her husband perceive this, she felt that, notwithstanding what had occurred, no friendship was broken between them; on the contrary, that he liked Lars very much.

The day for the parish meeting came. In the morning, Lars Hogstad drove over for Canute Aakre, who came out and took a seat beside him. They saluted each other as usual, spoke a little less than they were wont on the way, but not at all of the proposal. The meeting was full; some, too, had come in as spectators, which Canute did not like, for he perceived by this a little excitement in the parish. Lars had his straw, and stood by the stove, warming himself, for the autumn had begun to be cold. The chairman read the proposal in a subdued and careful manner, adding, that it came from the Foged, who was not habitually fortunate. The building was a gift, and such things it was not customary to part with, least of all when there was no necessity for it.

Lars, who never before had spoken in the meetings, to the surprise of all, took the floor. His voice trembled; whether this was caused by regard for Canute, or anxiety for the success of the bill, we cannot say; but his arguments were clear, good, and of such a comprehensive and compact character as had hardly before been heard in these meetings. In concluding, he said:

"Of what importance is it that the proposal is from the Foged?—none,— or who it was that erected the house, or in what way it became the public property?"

Canute, who blushed easily, turned very red, and moved nervously as usual when he was impatient; but notwithstanding, he answered in a low, careful tone, that there were savings banks enough in the country, he thought, quite near, and almost too near. But if one was to be instituted, there were other ways of attaining this end, than by trampling upon the gifts of the dead, and the love of the living. His voice was a little unsteady when he said this, but recovered its composure, when he began to speak of the grain magazine as such, and reason concerning its utility.

Lars answered him ably on this last, adding: "Besides, for many reasons I would be led to doubt whether the affairs of this parish are to be conducted for the best interests of the living, or for the memory of the dead; or further, whether it is the love and hate of a single family which rules, rather than the welfare of the whole."

Canute answered quickly: "I don't know whether the last speaker has been the one least benefited not only by the dead of this family, but also by its still living representative."

In this remark he aimed first at the fact that his powerful grandfather had, in his day, managed the farm for Lars' grandfather, when the latter, on his own account, was on a little visit to the penitentiary.

The straw, which had been moving quickly for a long time, was now still :

" I am not in the habit of speaking everywhere of myself and family," said he, treating the matter with calm superiority ; then he reviewed the whole matter in question, aiming throughout at a particular point. Canute was forced to acknowledge to himself, that he had never looked upon it from that standpoint, or heard such reasoning ; involuntarily he had to turn his eye upon Lars. There he stood tall and portly, with clearness marked upon the strongly-built forehead and in the deep eyes. His mouth was compressed, the straw still hung playing in its corner, but great strength lay around. He kept his hands behind him, standing erect, while his low deep intonations seemed as if from the ground in which he was rooted. Canute saw him for the first time in his life, and from his inmost soul felt a dread of him ; for unmistakably this man had always been his superior ! He had taken all Canute himself knew or could impart, but retained only what had nourished this strong hidden growth.

He had loved and cherished Lars, but now

that he had become a giant, he hated him deeply, fearfully; he could not explain to himself why he thought so, but he felt it instinctively, while gazing upon him; and in this forgetting all else, he exclaimed:

"But Lars! Lars! what in the Lord's name ails you?"

He lost all self-control,—"you, whom I have "—"you, who have "—he could n't get out another word, and seated himself, only to struggle against the excitement which he was unwilling to have Lars see; he drew himself up, struck the table with his fist, and his eyes snapped from below the stiff disorderly hair which always shaded them. Lars appeared as if he had not been interrupted, only turning his head to the assembly, asking if this should be considered the decisive blow in the matter, for in such a case nothing more need be said.

Canute could not endure this calmness.

"What is it that has come among us?" he cried. "Us, who to this day have never debated but in love and upright zeal? We are infuriated at each other as if incited by an evil spirit;" and he looked with fiery eyes upon Lars, who answered:

"You yourself surely bring in this spirit, Canute, for I have spoken only of the case. But you will look upon it only through your own self-will; now we shall see if your love and upright

zeal will endure, when once it is decided agree-
ably to our wish."

"Have I not, then, taken good care of the
interests of the parish?"

No reply.   This grieved Canute, and he continued:

"Really, I did not think otherwise than that
I had accomplished something;—something for
the good of the parish;—but may be I have
deceived myself."

He became excited again, for it was a fiery
spirit within him, which was broken in many
ways, and the parting with Lars grieved him, so
he could hardly control himself.   Lars answered:

"Yes, I know you give yourself the credit for
all that is done here, and should one judge by
much speaking in the meetings, then surely you
have accomplished the most.

"Oh, is it this!" shouted Canute, looking
sharply upon Lars: "it is you who have the
honor of it!"

"Since we necessarily talk of ourselves," replied Lars, "I will say that all matters have
been carefully considered by us before they were
introduced here."

Here little Canute Aakre resumed his quick
way of speaking:

"In God's name take the honor, I am content
to live without it; there are other things harder
to lose!"

Involuntarily Lars turned his eye from Canute, but said, the straw moving very quickly: "If I were to speak my mind, I should say there is not much to take honor for;—of course ministers and teachers may be satisfied with what has been done; but, certainly, the common men say only that up to this time the taxes have become heavier and heavier."

A murmur arose in the assembly, which now became restless.   Lars continued:

"Finally, to-day, a proposition is made which, if carried, would recompense the parish for all it has laid out; perhaps, for this reason, it meets such opposition.   It is the affair of the parish, for the benefit of all its inhabitants, and ought to be rescued from being a family matter."

The audience exchanged glances, and spoke half audibly, when one threw out a remark as he rose to go to his dinner-pail, that these were "the truest words he had heard in the meetings for many years."   Now all arose, and the conversation became general.   Canute Aakre felt as he sat there that the case was lost, fearfully lost; and tried no more to save it.   He had somewhat of the character attributed to Frenchmen, in that he was good for first, second, and third attacks, but poor for self-defence—his sensibilities overpowering his thoughts.

He could not comprehend it, nor could he sit quietly any longer; so, yielding his place to the vice-chairman, he left,—and the audience smiled.

He had come to the meeting accompanied by Lars, but returned home alone, though the road was long. It was a cold autumn day; the way looked jagged and bare, the meadow gray and yellow; while frost had begun to appear here and there on the roadside. Disappointment is a dreadful companion. He felt himself so small and desolate, walking there; but Lars was everywhere before him, like a giant, his head towering, in the dusk of evening, to the sky. It was his own fault that this had been the decisive battle, and the thought grieved him sorely: he had staked too much upon a single little affair. But surprise, pain, anger, had mastered him; his heart still burned, shrieked, and moaned within him. He heard the rattling of a wagon behind; it was Lars, who came driving his superb horse past him at a brisk trot, so that the hard road gave a sound of thunder. Canute gazed after him, as he sat there so broad-shouldered in the wagon, while the horse, impatient for home, hurried on unurged by Lars, who only gave loose rein. It was a picture of his power; this man drove toward the mark! He, Canute, felt as if thrown out of his wagon to stagger along there in the autumn cold.

Canute's wife was waiting for him at home. She knew there would be a battle; she had never

in her life believed in Lars, and lately had felt a
dread of him. It had been no comfort to her
that they had ridden away together, nor would
it have comforted her if they had returned in the
same way. But darkness had fallen, and they
had not yet come. She stood in the doorway,
went down the road and home again; but no
wagon appeared. At last she hears a rattling
on the road, her heart beats as violently as the
wheels revolve; she clings to the doorpost, looking out; the wagon is coming; only one sits
there; she recognizes Lars, who sees and recognizes her, but is driving past without stopping.
Now she is thoroughly alarmed! Her limbs fail
her; she staggers in, sinking on the bench by the
window. The children, alarmed, gather around,
the youngest asking for papa, for the mother
never spoke with them but of him. She loved
him because he had such a good heart, and now
this good heart was not with them; but, on the
contrary, away on all kinds of business, which
brought him only unhappiness; consequently,
they were unhappy too.

"Oh, that no harm had come to him to-day!
Canute was so excitable! Why did Lars come
home alone? why did n't he stop?"

Should she run after him, or, in the opposite
direction, toward her husband? She felt faint,
and the children pressed around her, asking what
was the matter; but this could not be told to

7

them, so she said they must take supper alone,
and, rising, arranged it and helped them. She
was constantly glancing out upon the road. He
did not come. She undressed and put them to
bed, and the youngest repeated the evening
prayer, while she bowed over him, praying so fer-
vently in the words which the tiny mouth first uttered, that she did not perceive the steps outside.

Canute stood in the doorway, gazing upon his
little congregation at prayer. She rose; all the
children shouted "Papa!" but he seated himself, and said gently:

"Oh! let him repeat it."

The mother turned again to the bedside, that
meantime he might not see her face; otherwise,
it would have been like intermeddling with his
grief before he felt a necessity of revealing it.
The child folded its hands,—the rest followed
the example,—and it said:

"I am now a little lad,
    But soon shall grow up tall,
    And make papa and mamma glad,
    I'll be so good to all!
    When in Thy true and holy ways,
    Thou dear, dear God wilt help me keep;—
    Remember now Thy name to praise
    And so we'll try to go to sleep!"

What a peace now fell! Not a minute more
had passed ere the children all slept in it as in
the lap of God; but the mother went quietly to

work arranging supper for the father, who as yet could not eat. But after he had gone to bed, he said:

"Now, after this, I shall be at home."

The mother lay there, trembling with joy, not daring to speak, lest she should reveal it; and she thanked God for all that had happened, for, whatever it was, it had resulted in good.

II.

In the course of a year, Lars was chosen head Justice of the Peace, chairman of the board of commissioners, president of the savings-bank, and, in short, was placed in every office of parish trust to which his election was possible. In the county legislature, during the first year, he remained silent, but afterward made himself as conspicuous as in the parish council; for here, too, stepping up to the contest with him who had always borne sway, he was victorious over the whole line, and afterward himself manager. From this he was elected to the Congress, where his fame had preceded him, and he found no lack of challenge. But here, although steady and independent, he was always retiring, never venturing beyond his depth, lest his post as leader at home should be endangered by a possible defeat abroad.

It was pleasant to him now in his own town.

When he stood by the church-wall on Sundays, and the community glided past, saluting and glancing sideways at him,—now and then one stepping up for the honor of exchanging a couple of words with him,—it could almost be said that, standing there, he controlled the whole parish with a straw, which, of course, hung in the corner of his mouth.

He deserved his popularity ; for he had opened a new road which led to the church ; all this and much more resulted from the savings-bank, which he had instituted and now managed ; and the parish, in its self-management and good order, was held up as an example to all others.

Canute, of his own accord, quite withdrew,— not entirely at first, for he had promised himself not thus to yield to pride. In the first proposal he made before the parish board, he became entangled by Lars, who would have it represented in all its details ; and, somewhat hurt, he replied : "When Columbus discovered America he did not have it divided into counties and towns, —this came by degrees afterward ; " upon which, Lars compared Canute's proposition (relating to stable improvements) to the discovery of America, and afterward by the commissioners he was called by no other name than "Discovery of America." Canute thought since his influence had ceased there, so, also, had his duty to work ; and afterwards declined re-election.

But he was industrious, and, in order still to do something for the public good, he enlarged his Sunday-school, and put it, by means of small contributions from the pupils, in connection with the mission cause, of which he soon became the centre and leader in his own and surrounding counties.   At this, Lars remarked that, if Canute ever wished to collect money for any purpose, he must first know that its benefit was only to be realized some thousands of miles away.

There was no strife between them now.   True, they associated with each other no longer, but saluted and exchanged a few words whenever they met.   Canute always felt a little pain in remembering Lars, but struggled to overcome it, by saying to himself that it must have been so. Many years afterward at a large wedding-party, where both were present and a little gay, Canute stepped upon a chair and proposed a toast to the chairman of the parish council, and the county's first congressman.   He spoke until he manifested emotion, and, as usual, in an exceedingly handsome way.   It was honorably done, and Lars came to him, saying, with an unsteady eye, that for much of what he knew and was, he had to thank him.

At the next election, Canute was again elected chairman.

But if Lars Hogstad had foreseen what was to follow, he would not have influenced this.   It is

a saying that "all events happen in their time,"
and just as Canute appeared again in the council, the ablest men in the parish were threatened
with bankruptcy, the result of a speculative fever
which had been raging long, but now first began
to react. They said that Lars Hogstad had
caused this great epidemic, for it was he who
had brought the spirit of speculation into the parish. This penny malady had originated in the
parish board; for this body itself had acted as
leading speculator.   Down to the youth of twenty
years, all were endeavoring by sharp bargains to
make the one dollar, ten; extreme parsimony, in
order to lay up in the beginning, was followed by
an exceeding lavishness in the end: and as the
thoughts of all were directed to money only, a
disposition to selfishness, suspicion, and disunion
had developed itself, which at last turned to prosecutions and hatred.   It was said that the parish board had set the example in this also; for
one of the first acts, performed by Lars as chairman, was a prosecution against the minister, concerning doubtful prerogatives. The venerable
pastor had lost, but had also immediately re-
signed.   At the time some had praised, others
denounced, this act of Lars; but it had proved
a bad example. Now came the effects of his
management in the form of loss to all the leading men of the parish; and consequently, the
public opinion quickly changed.   The opposite

party immediately found a champion; for Canute
Aakre had come into the parish board,—introduced there by Lars himself.

The struggle at once began.   All those youths,
who, in their time, had been under Canute
Aakre's instruction, were now grown-up men, the
best educated, conversant with all the business
and public transactions in the parish; Lars had
now to contend against these and others like
them, who had disliked him from their child-
hood.   One evening after a stormy debate, as he
stood on the platform outside his door, looking
over the parish, a sound of distant threatening
thunder came toward him from the large farms,
lying in the storm.   He knew that that day their
owners had become insolvent, that he himself
and the savings-bank were going the same way:
and his whole long work would culminate in con-
demnation against him.

In these days of struggle and despair, a company of surveyors came one evening to Hogstad,
which was the first farm at the entrance of the
parish to mark out the line of a new railroad.
In the course of conversation, Lars perceived it
was still a question with them whether the road
should run through this valley, or another par-
allel one.

Like a flash of lightning it darted through his
mind, that, if he could manage to get it through
here, all real estate would rise in value, and not

only he himself be saved, but his popularity handed down to future generations. He could not sleep that night, for his eyes were dazzled with visions; sometimes he seemed to hear the noise of an engine. The next day he accompanied the surveyors in their examination of the locality; his horses carried them, and to his farm they returned. The following day they drove through the other valley, he still with them, and again carrying them back home. The whole house was illuminated, the first men of the parish having been invited to a party made for the surveyors, which terminated in a carouse that lasted until morning. But to no avail; for the nearer they came to the decision, the clearer it was to be seen that the road could not be built through here without great extra expense. The entrance to the valley was narrow, through a rocky chasm, and the moment it swung into the parish the river made a curve in its way, so that the road would either have to make the same—crossing the river twice—or go straight forward through the old, now unused, churchyard. But it was not long since the last burials there, for the church had been but recently moved.

Did it only depend upon a strip of an old churchyard, thought Lars, whether the parish should have this great blessing or not?—then he would use his name and energy for the removal of the obstacle. So immediately he made a

visit to minister and bishop, from them to county
legislature and Department of the Interior; he
reasoned and negotiated; for he had possessed
himself of all possible information concerning
the vast profits that would accrue on the one
side, and the feelings of the parish on the other,
and had really succeeded in gaining over all par-
ties.   It was promised him that by the reinter-
ment of some bodies in the new churchyard, the
only objection to this line might be considered
as removed, and the king's approbation guar-
anteed.   It was told him that he need only make
the motion in the county meeting.

The parish had become as excited on the
question as himself.   The spirit of speculation,
which had been prevalent so many years, now
became jubilant.   No one spoke or thought of
anything but Lars' journey and its probable result.   Consequently, when he returned with the
most splendid promises, they made much ado
about him; songs were sung to his praise,—yes,
if at that time one after another of the largest
farms had toppled over, not a soul would have
given it any attention; the former speculation
fever had been succeeded by the new one of the
railroad.

The county board met; an humble petition
that the old churchyard might be used for the
railroad was drawn up to be presented to the
king.   This was unanimously voted; yes, there

was even talk of voting thanks to Lars, and a
gift of a coffee-pot, in the model of a locomotive.
But finally, it was thought best to wait until
everything was accomplished. The petition
from the parish to the county board was sent
back, with a requirement of a list of the names
of all bodies which must necessarily be removed.
The minister made out this, but instead of send-
ing it directly to the county board, had his
reasons for communicating it first to the parish.
One of the members brought it to the next meeting. Here, Lars opened the envelope, and as
chairman read the names.

Now it happened that the first body to be removed was that of Lars' own grandfather. A
little shudder passed through the assembly; Lars
himself was taken by surprise; but continued.
Secondly, came the name of Canute Aakre's
grandfather; for the two had died at nearly the
same time. Canute Aakre sprang from his seat;
Lars stopped; all looked up with dread; for the
name of the elder Canute Aakre had been the
one most beloved in the parish for generations.
There was a pause of some minutes. At last
Lars hemmed, and continued. But the matter
became worse, for the further he proceeded, the
nearer it approached their own day, and the
dearer the dead became. When he ceased,
Canute Aakre asked quietly if others did not
think as he, that spirits were around them. It

had begun to grow dusk in the room, and although they were mature men sitting in company, they almost felt themselves frightened. Lars took a bundle of matches from his pocket and lit a candle, somewhat dryly remarking that this was no more than they had known beforehand.

"No," replied Canute, pacing the floor, "this is more than I knew beforehand. Now I begin to think that even railroads can be bought too dearly."

This electrified the audience, and Canute continued that the whole affair must be reconsidered, and made a motion to that effect. In the excitement which had prevailed, he said it was also true that the benefit to be derived from the road had been considerably overrated; for if it did not pass through the parish, there would have to be a depot at each extremity; true, it would be a little more trouble to drive there, than to a station within; yet not so great as that for this reason they should dishonor the rest of the dead. Canute was one of those who, when his thoughts were excited, could extemporize and present most sound reasons; he had not a moment previously thought of what he now said; but the truth of it struck all. Lars, seeing the danger of his position, thought best to be careful, and so apparently acquiesced in Canute's proposition to reconsider; for such emotions, thought he, are always strongest in the beginning; one must temporize with them.

But here he had miscalculated. In constantly increasing waves the dread of touching their dead overswept the parish; what no one had thought of as long as the matter existed only in talk became a serious question when it came to touch themselves. The women particularly were excited, and at the parish house, on the day of the next meeting, the road was black with the gathered multitude. It was a warm summer day, the windows were taken out, and as many stood without as within. All felt that that day would witness a great battle.

Lars came, driving his handsome horse, saluted by all; he looked quietly and confidently around, not seeming surprised at the throng. He seated himself, straw in mouth, near the window, and not without a smile saw Canute rise to speak, as he thought, for all the dead lying over there in the old churchyard.

But Canute Aakre did not begin with the churchyard. He made a stricter investigation into the profits likely to accrue from carrying the road through the parish, showing that in all this excitement they had been over-estimated. He had calculated the distance of each farm from the nearest station, should the road be taken through the neighboring valley, and finally asked:

"Why has such a hurrah been made about this railroad, when it would not be for the good of the parish after all?"

This he could explain; there were those who had brought about such a previous disturbance, that a greater was necessary in order that the first might be forgotten. Then, too, there were those who, while the thing was new, could sell their farms and lands to strangers, foolish enough to buy; it was a shameful speculation, which not the living only but the dead also must be made to promote!

The effect produced by his address was very considerable. But Lars had firmly resolved, come what would, to keep cool, and smilingly replied that he supposed Canute Aakre himself had been anxious for the railroad, and surely no one would accuse him of understanding speculation. (A little laugh ensued.) Canute had had no objection to the removal of bodies of common people for the sake of the railroad, but when it came to that of his own grandfather, the question became suddenly of vital importance to the whole parish. He said no more, but looked smilingly at Canute, as did also several others. Meanwhile, Canute Aakre surprised both him and them by replying:

"I confess it; I did not realize what was at stake until it touched my own dead; possibly this is a shame, but really it would have been a greater one not even then to have realized it, as is the case with Lars! Never, I think, could Lars' raillery have been more out of place; for folks with common feelings the thing is really revolting."

"This feeling has come up quite recently," answered Lars, "and so we will hope for its speedy disappearance also. It may be well to think upon what minister, bishop, county officers, engineers, and Department will say, if we first unanimously set the ball in motion and then come asking to have it stopped; if we first are jubilant and sing songs, then weep and chant requiems. If they do not say that we have run mad here in the parish, at least they may say that we have grown a little queer lately."

"Yes, God knows, they can say so," answered Canute; "we have been acting strangely enough during the last few days,—it is time for us to retract. It has really gone far when we can dig up, each his own grandfather, to make way for a railroad; when in order that our loads may be carried more easily forward, we can violate the resting-place of the dead. For is not overhauling our churchyard the same as making it yield us food? What has been buried there in Jesus' name, shall we take up in the name of Mammon? It is but little better than eating our progenitors' bones."

"That is according to the order of nature," said Lars dryly.

"Yes, the nature of plants and animals," replied Canute.

"Are we not then animals?" asked Lars.

"Yes, but also the children of the living God, who have buried our dead in faith upon Him; it is He who shall raise them, and not we."

"Oh, you prate! Are not the graves dug over at certain fixed periods anyway? What evil is there in that it happens some years earlier?" asked Lars.

"I will tell you! What was born of them yet lives; what they built yet remains; what they loved, taught, and suffered for is all around us and within us; and shall we not, then, let their bodies rest in peace?"

"I see by your warmth that you are thinking of your grandfather again," replied Lars; "and will say it is high time you ceased to bother the parish about him, for he monopolized space enough in his lifetime; it is n't worth while to have him lie in the way now he is dead. Should his corpse prevent a blessing to the parish that would reach to a hundred generations, we surely would have reason to say, that of all born here he has done us most harm."

Canute Aakre tossed back his disorderly hair, his eyes darted fire, his whole frame appeared like a drawn bow.

"What sort of a blessing this is that you speak of, I have already proved. It is of the same

character as all the others which you have
brought to the parish, namely, a doubtful one.
True enough you have provided us with a new
church; but, too, you have filled it with a new
spirit,—and not that of love. True, you have
made us new roads,—but also new roads to de-
struction, as is now plainly evident in the mis-
fortunes of many. True, you have lessened our
taxes to the public; but, too, you have increased
those to ourselves;—prosecutions, protests, and
failures are no blessing to a community. And
you dare scoff at the man in his grave whom the
whole parish blesses! You dare say he lies in
our way,—yes, very likely he lies in your way.
This is plainly to be seen; but over this grave
you shall fall! The spirit which has reigned
over you, and at the same time until now over
us, was not born to rule, only to serve. The
churchyard shall surely remain undisturbed;
but to-day it numbers one more grave, namely,
that of your popularity, which shall now be in-
terred in it."

Lars Hogstad rose, white as a sheet; he opened
his mouth, but was unable to speak a word, and
the straw fell. After three or four vain attempts
to recover it and to find utterance, he belched
forth like a volcano:

"Are these the thanks I get for all my toils
and struggles? Shall such a woman-preacher be
able to direct? Ah, then, the devil be your

chairman if ever more I set my foot here!   I have kept your petty business in order until to-day; and after me it will fall into a thousand pieces; but let it go now.   Here are the ' Records!' (and he flung them across the table).   Out on such a company of wenches and brats! (striking the table with his fist).   Out on the whole parish, that it can see a man recompensed as I now am!"

He brought down his fist once more with such force, that the leaf of the great table sprang upward, and the inkstand with all its contents downward upon the floor, marking for coming generations the spot where Lars Hogstad, in spite of all his prudence, lost his patience and his rule.

He sprang for the door, and soon after was away from the house.   The whole audience stood fixed,—for the power of his voice and his wrath had frightened them,—until Canute Aakre, remembering the taunt he had received at the time of his fall, with beaming countenance, and assuming Lars' voice, exclaimed:

" Is this the decisive blow in the matter?"

The assembly burst into uproarious merriment. The grave meeting closed amid laughter, talk, and high glee; only few left the place, those remaining called for drink, and made a night of thunder succeed a day of lightning.   They felt happy and independent as in old days, before the time in which the commanding spirit of Lars

8

had cowed their souls into silent obedience.
They drank toasts to their liberty, they sang,
yes, finally they danced, Canute Aakre with the
vice-chairman taking lead, and all the members
of the council following, and boys and girls too,
while the young ones outside shouted, "hurrah!"
for such a spectacle they had never before wit-
nessed.

III.

LARS moved around in the large rooms at
Hogstad without uttering a word.   His wife who
loved him, but always with fear and trembling,
dared not so much as show herself in his presence.
The management of the farm and house had
to go on as it would, while a multitude of letters
were passing to and fro between Hogstad and the
parish, Hogstad and the capital; for he had
charges against the county board which were
not acknowledged, and a prosecution ensued;
against the savings-bank, which were also unac-
knowledged, and so came another prosecution.
He took offence at articles in the *Christiania
Correspondence*, and prosecuted again, first the
chairman of the county board, and then the di-
rectors of the savings-bank.   At the same time
there were bitter articles in the papers, which
according to report were by him, and were the
cause of great strife in the parish, setting neigh-

bor against neighbor. Sometimes he was absent whole weeks at once, nobody knowing where, and after returning lived secluded as before. At church he was not seen after the grand scene in the representatives' meeting.

Then, one Saturday night, the mail brought news that the railroad was to go through the parish after all, and through the old churchyard. It struck like lightning into every home. The unanimous veto of the county board had been in vain; Lars Hogstad's influence had proved stronger. This was what his absence meant, this was his work! It was involuntary on the part of the people that admiration of the man and his dogged persistency should lessen dissatisfaction at their own defeat; and the more they talked of the matter the more reconciled they seemed to become: for whatever has once been settled beyond all change develops in itself, little by little, reasons why it is so, which we are accordingly brought to acknowledge.

In going to church next day, as they encountered each other they could not help laughing; and before the service, just as nearly all were convened outside,—young and old, men and women, yes, even children,—talking about Lars Hogstad, his talents, his strong will, and his great influence, he himself with his household came driving up in four carriages. Two years had passed since he was last there. He alighted

and walked through the crowd, when involuntarily all lifted their hats to him like one man ;
but he looked neither to the right nor the left, nor
returned a single salutation.   His little wife, pale
as death, walked behind him.   In the house, the
surprise became so great that, one after another,
noticing him, stopped singing and stared.   Canute Aakre, who sat in his pew in front of Lars',
perceiving the unusual appearance and no cause
for it in front, turned around and saw Lars sitting bowed over his hymn-book, looking for the
place.

He had not seen him until now since the
day of the representatives' meeting, and such a
change in a man he never could have imagined.
This was no victor. His head was becoming
bald, his face was lean and contracted, his eyes
hollow and bloodshot, and the giant neck presented wrinkles and cords.   At a glance he perceived what this man had endured, and was as
suddenly seized with a feeling of strong pity,
yes, even with a touch of the old love.   In his
heart he prayed for him, and promised himself
surely to seek him after service ; but, ere he had
opportunity, Lars had gone.   Canute resolved
he would call upon him at his home that night,
but his wife kept him back.

"Lars is one of the kind," said she, " who
cannot endure a debt of gratitude : keep away
from him until possibly he can in some way do

you a favor, and then perhaps he will come to
you."

However, he did not come. He appeared
now and then at church, but nowhere else, and
associated with no one. On the contrary, he
devoted himself to his farm and other business
with an earnestness which showed a determina-
tion to make up in one year for the neglect of
many; and, too, there were those who said it
was necessary.

Railroad operations in the valley began very
soon. As the line was to go directly past his
house, Lars remodelled the side facing the road,
connecting with it an elegant verandah, for of
course his residence must attract attention. They
were just engaged in this work when the rails
were laid for the conveyance of gravel and
timber, and a small locomotive was brought up.
It was a fine autumn evening when the first
gravel train was to come down. Lars stood on
the platform of his house to hear the first signal, and see the first column of smoke; all the
hands on the farm were gathered around him.
He looked out over the parish, lying in the setting sun, and felt that he was to be remembered
so long as a train should roar through the fruit-
ful valley. A feeling of forgiveness crept into
his soul. He looked toward the churchyard, of
which a part remained, with crosses bowing toward the earth, but a part had become railroad.

He was just trying to define his feelings, when, whistle went the first signal, and a while after the train came slowly along, puffing out smoke mingled with sparks, for wood was used instead of coal; the wind blew toward the house, and standing there they soon found themselves enveloped in a dense smoke; but by and by, as it cleared away, Lars saw the train working through the valley like a strong will.

He was satisfied, and entered the house as after a long day's work. The image of his grandfather stood before him at this moment. This grandfather had raised the family from poverty to forehanded circumstances; true, a part of his citizen-honor had been lost, but forward he had pushed, nevertheless. His faults were those of his time; they were to be found on the uncertain borders of the moral conceptions of that period, and are of no consideration now. Honor to him in his grave, for he suffered and worked; peace to his ashes. It is good to rest at last. But he could get no rest because of his grandson's great ambition. He was thrown up with stone and gravel. Pshaw! very likely he would only smile that his grandson's work passed above his head.

With such thoughts he had undressed and gone to bed. Again his grandfather's image glided forth. What did he wish. Surely he ought to be satisfied now, with the family's honor sounding forth above his grave; who else had such a

monument? But yet, what mean these two great
eyes of fire? This hissing, roaring, is no longer
the locomotive, for see! it comes from the
churchyard directly toward the house: an im-
mense procession! The eyes of fire are his
grandfather's, and the train behind are all the
dead. It advances continually toward the house,
roaring, crackling, flashing. The windows burn
in the reflection of dead men's eyes . . . he made
a mighty effort to collect himself, "For it was a
dream, of course, only a dream; but let me
waken! . . . See: now I am awake; come,
ghosts!"

And behold: they really come from the churchyard, overthrowing road, rails, locomotive and
train with such violence that they sink in the
ground; and then all is still there, covered with
sod and crosses as before. But like giants the
spirits advanced, and the hymn, "Let the dead
have rest!" goes before them. He knows it;
for daily in all these years it has sounded through
his soul, and now it becomes his own requiem;
for this was death and its visions. The perspira-
tion started out over his whole body, for nearer
and nearer,—and see there, on the window-pane!
there, there they are now; and he heard his name.
Overpowered with dread he struggled to shout,
for he was strangling; a dead, cold hand already
clenched his throat, when he regained his voice
in a shrieking "Help me!" and awoke. At that

moment the window was burst in with such force
that the pieces flew on to his bed. He sprang
up ; a man stood in the opening, around him
smoke and tongues of fire.

"The house is burning, Lars, we'll help you
out ! "

It was Canute Aakre.

When again he recovered consciousness, he
was lying out in a piercing wind that chilled his
limbs. No one was by him ; on the left he saw
his burning house ; around him grazed, bellowed,
bleated, and neighed his stock ; the sheep hud-
dled together in a terrified flock ; the furniture
recklessly scattered : but, on looking around
more carefully, he discovered somebody sitting
on a knoll near him, weeping. It was his wife.
He called her name. She started.

"The Lord Jesus be thanked that you live,"
she exclaimed, coming forward and seating herself, or rather falling down before him : " O God !
O God ! now we have enough of that railroad ! "

"The railroad ?" he asked : but ere he spoke,
it had flashed through his mind how it was ; for,
of course, the cause of the fire was the falling of
sparks from the locomotive among the shavings
by the new side-wall. He remained sitting, silent
and thoughtful ; his wife dared say no more,
but was trying to find clothes for him : the things
with which she had covered him, as he lay un-
conscious, having fallen off. He received her

attentions in silence, but as she crouched down
to cover his feet, he laid a hand upon her head.
She hid her face in his lap, and wept aloud.   At
last he had noticed her.   Lars understood, and
said :

"You are the only friend I have."

Although to hear these words had cost the
house, no matter, they made her happy ; she
gathered courage and said, rising and looking
submissively at him :

"That is because no one else understands
you."

Now again they talked of all that had trans-
pired, or rather he remained silent, while she told
about it.   Canute Aakre had been first to perceive the fire, had awakened his people, sent the
girls out through the parish, while he himself
hastened with men and horses to the spot where
all were sleeping.   He had taken charge of extin-
guishing the fire and saving the property ; Lars
himself he had dragged from the burning room
and brought him here on the left, to the wind-
ward,—here, out on the churchyard.

While they were talking of all this, some one
came driving rapidly up the road and turned off
toward them; soon he alighted.   It was Canute,
who had been home after his church-wagon ; the
one in which so many times they had ridden
together to and from the parish meetings.   Now
Lars must get in and ride home with him.   They

took each other by the hand, one sitting, the other standing.

"You must come with me now," said Canute. Without reply Lars rose : they walked side by side to the wagon. Lars was helped in : Canute seated himself by his side. What they talked about as they rode, or afterward in the little chamber at Aakre, in which they remained until morning, has never been known ; but from that day they were again inseparable.

As soon as disaster befalls a man, all seem to understand his worth. So the parish took upon themselves to rebuild Lars Hogstad's houses, larger and handsomer than any others in the valley. Again he became chairman, but with Canute Aakre at his side, and from that day all went well.

THE FATHER

BY

BJÖRNSTJERNE BJÖRNSON

Translated by Prof. R. B. Anderson.

THE FATHER

BY BJÖRNSTJERNE BJÖRNSON

THE man whose story is here to be told was the wealthiest and most influential person in his parish; his name was Thord Overaas. He appeared in the priest's study one day, tall and earnest.

"I have gotten a son," said he, "and I wish to present him for baptism."

"What shall his name be?"

"Finn,—after my father."

"And the sponsors?"

They were mentioned, and proved to be the best men and women of Thord's relations in the parish.

"Is there anything else?" inquired the priest, and looked up.

The peasant hesitated a little.

"I should like very much to have him baptized by himself," said he, finally.

"That is to say on a week-day?"

"Next Saturday, at twelve o'clock noon."

"Is there anything else?" inquired the priest.

"There is nothing else;" and the peasant twirled his cap, as though he were about to go.

Then the priest rose. "There is yet this, however," said he, and walking toward Thord, he took him by the hand and looked gravely into his eyes: "God grant that the child may become a blessing to you!"

One day sixteen years later, Thord stood once more in the priest's study.

"Really, you carry your age astonishingly well, Thord," said the priest; for he saw no change whatever in the man.

"That is because I have no troubles," replied Thord.

To this the priest said nothing, but after a while he asked: "What is your pleasure this evening?"

"I have come this evening about that son of mine who is to be confirmed to-morrow."

"He is a bright boy."

"I did not wish to pay the priest until I heard what number the boy would have when he takes his place in church to-morrow."

"He will stand number one.'

"So I have heard; and here are ten dollars for the priest."

"Is there anything else I can do for you?" inquired the priest, fixing his eyes on Thord.

"There is nothing else."

Thord went out.

Eight years more rolled by, and then one day a noise was heard outside of the priest's study, for many men were approaching, and at their head was Thord, who entered first.

The priest looked up and recognized him.

"You come well attended this evening, Thord," said he.

"I am here to request that the banns may be published for my son; he is about to marry Karen Storliden, daughter of Gudmund, who stands here beside me."

"Why, that is the richest girl in the parish."

"So they say," replied the peasant, stroking back his hair with one hand.

The priest sat a while as if in deep thought, then entered the names in his book, without making any comments, and the men wrote their signatures underneath. Thord laid three dollars on the table.

"One is all I am to have," said the priest.

"I know that very well; but he is my only child, I want to do it handsomely."

The priest took the money.

"This is now the third time, Thord, that you have come here on your son's account."

"But now I am through with him," said Thord, and folding up his pocket-book he said farewell and walked away.

The men slowly followed him.

A fortnight later, the father and son were

rowing across the lake, one calm, still day, to
Storliden to make arrangements for the wedding.

"This thwart is not secure," said the son,
and stood up to straighten the seat on which he
was sitting.

At the same moment the board he was standing on slipped from under him; he threw out his
arms, uttered a shriek, and fell overboard.

"Take hold of the oar!" shouted the father,
springing to his feet and holding out the oar.

But when the son had made a couple of efforts
he grew stiff.

"Wait a moment!" cried the father, and began
to row toward his son.

Then the son rolled over on his back, gave his
father one long look, and sank.

Thord could scarcely believe it; he held the
boat still, and stared at the spot where his son
had gone down, as though he must surely come
to the surface again. There rose some bubbles,
then some more, and finally one large one that
burst; and the lake lay there as smooth and
bright as a mirror again.

For three days and three nights people saw
the father rowing round and round the spot,
without taking either food or sleep; he was
dragging the lake for the body of his son. And
toward morning of the third day he found it, and
carried it in his arms up over the hills to his gard.

It might have been about a year from that day,

when the priest, late one autumn evening, heard some one in the passage outside of the door, carefully trying to find the latch. The priest opened the door, and in walked a tall, thin man, with bowed form and white hair. The priest looked long at him before he recognized him. It was Thord.

"Are you out walking so late?" said the priest, and stood still in front of him.

"Ah, yes! it is late," said Thord, and took a seat.

The priest sat down also, as though waiting. A long, long silence followed. At last Thord said:

"I have something with me that I should like to give to the poor; I want it to be invested as a legacy in my son's name."

He rose, laid some money on the table, and sat down again. The priest counted it.

"It is a great deal of money," said he.

"It is half the price of my gard. I sold it to-day."

The priest sat long in silence. At last he asked, but gently:

"What do you propose to do now, Thord?"

"Something better."

They sat there for a while, Thord with down-cast eyes, the priest with his eyes fixed on Thord. Presently the priest said, slowly and softly:

3

"I think your son has at last brought you a true blessing."

"Yes, I think so myself," said Thord, looking up, while two big tears coursed slowly down his cheeks.